KIDS HAVE FEELINGS, TOO

Mom and Dad Break Up

By Joan Singleton Prestine

Illustrations by Virginia Kylberg

McGraw-Hill
Children's Publishing

McGraw-Hill
Children's Publishing
A Division of The McGraw·Hill Companies

Send all inquiries to:
McGraw-Hill Children's Publishing
8787 Orion Place
Columbus, OH 43240-4027

ISBN 1-57768-683-7

Library of Congress Cataloging-in-Publication Data is on file with the publisher.

Printed in the United States of America.

1 2 3 4 5 6 7 8 9 PHXBK 01 02 03 04 05 06 07 08 09

Some things belong together.
Peanut butter and jelly.
Bees and honey. Mom and Dad.

Some things belong apart.
The sun and moon. Summer and winter.
Weeds and flowers.

But sometimes things
that belong together,
like Mom and Dad, break up.

That's not the way it's supposed to be. Sometimes I feel mad. I yell at my friends to go away and I pound my pillow.

Sometimes I feel sad. My friend Anthony wants me to go ice skating. But all I want to do is cry.

Sometimes I feel lonely,
even when I'm with my friends.

Sometimes I dream that
Mom and Dad didn't break up.

I dream that we're all at home the way it's supposed to be— happy and together. But then I wake up and realize it was a dream.

Even though I know it wasn't my fault that Mom and Dad broke up, sometimes I feel like it was.

So I try to put
our family back together.
I make surprise parties
with cookies and juice.

I even pretend I am sick and need both of them to make me better. But nothing works. Sometimes things that belong together, like Mom and Dad, break up. And sometimes no one, not even me, can fix them.

N ow there's
Mom and me.
We ride bikes.

We draw
pictures for each other.
We talk.

And there's
Dad and me.
We play.

We read to each other.
We talk.

26

We don't all live together anymore.
But I know my Mom will always be my Mom.
And we'll have hugs.

And my Dad
will always be my Dad.
And we'll have hugs.

Discussing **Mom and Dad Break Up** with Children

After reading the story, encourage discussion. Children learn from sharing their thoughts and feelings.

Discussion Questions for **Mom and Dad Break Up**

- How did the boy feel when his parents were breaking up? What words describe his feelings?
- How did he show what he was feeling? What did he do?
- Why did the boy feel lonely when he had friends to play with?
- Why did he feel his parents' divorce was his fault even though he knew it wasn't?
- How did things work out in the end? What did the boy learn?
- What did the boy and his Mom enjoy doing together? What did the boy and his Dad enjoy doing together?

Significance of **Mom and Dad Break Up** for Children

Sometimes a book will trigger strong feelings in young children, especially if they have experienced a similar situation. If they feel comfortable, encourage children to share their experiences.